The PUFFIN PORTAL

VASHTI HARDY

With illustrations by
Natalie Smillie

For Poppy

First published in 2021 in Great Britain by
Barrington Stoke Ltd
18 Walker Street, Edinburgh, EH3 7LP

www.barringtonstoke.co.uk

Text © 2021 Vashti Hardy
Illustrations © 2021 Natalie Smillie

A CIP catalogue record for this book is available from the British Library upon request

ISBN: 978-1-78112-981-4

Printed by Hussar Books, Poland

CONTENTS

1

Mysterious Thefts

Bright blue crackling light blazed around Grace Griffin as she teleported back to the map room of Griffin House. She'd been to visit Mr Minnow in Carp Cove after he'd reported a theft.

"That was a short trip," said Watson, the family robot raven. He was perched on the back of an armchair.

Grace nodded. "It was yet another strange theft with no clear evidence or suspects." She gazed at the Griffin map, which was laid out on a huge table in the centre of the room. They'd had lots of calls about small thefts lately, and not just in Carp Cove.

Grace, her brother and their mum were wardens of the Griffin map, an amazing invention that allowed them to teleport across the whole of Moreland. Great Grandma Griffin had created the map years ago. She'd wanted to find a way to travel to even the most remote places in Moreland when people needed help.

The map showed the entire country with its many towns and villages, each with its own electrical gate. The gates were portals, letting the wardens teleport into the map. The Griffin family answered calls for help and played a part in ensuring life in Moreland ran smoothly. If a gate flashed red, it was an emergency call, and flashing blue meant it was a smaller problem.

As the youngest in the family, Grace took the blue calls and left the emergency ones to Mum and her brother, Bren. But Grace didn't mind. So many blue calls were coming in lately that her feet barely touched the ground in her home city of Copperport.

Grace placed a pocket-sized device on the map table. It was the re-compass that teleported her back home.

"So what did Mr Minnow say?" asked Watson, flying to land beside Grace.

She shrugged. "His spanner had gone missing. Once again, there were no fingerprints at the scene. Oh, and Mr Minnow said something strange about a puffin 'lurking' outside his shop."

"A puffin?" Watson squawked.

Grace frowned. "It doesn't make much sense, does it? None of the thefts do. The things being stolen don't have much value. If you were a thief, wouldn't you at least take more than one object at a time if you were going to the trouble of sneaking in to places without leaving fingerprints? Why is each theft so small – just one item?"

"Perhaps it's a nervous thief?" Watson suggested.

Grace shrugged again. "It's been the same for all the calls I've answered lately: a missing loaf of bread, glue, a pint of milk and now a spanner. They're all small thefts. I can't help but think they must be connected."

"Grace, you said yourself last time that old Mr Minnow seemed a bit scatty," Watson said. "He probably just mislaid the spanner."

"Maybe," Grace replied. "Didn't Mr Minnow accuse a bird of stealing something a few weeks back?"

The cogs in Watson's brain whirred, then he opened his mouth. Watson was able to replay recordings of things he'd heard people say, and that was what he did now. "You won't

believe the call I've just been on, Watson."
Grace's voice came out of Watson's mouth.
"Mr Minnow at Carp Cove says a bird stole a
jar of jam from his shop!"

Grace laughed. "Listening to myself is worse
than when you play back Mum's rules! But you're
right, Watson. Listening back, it does sound a bit
daft. Maybe Mr Minnow is not so reliable."

Watson flapped his mechanical wings and
flew a loop of the map table, circling Moreland.
"We have no evidence that the thefts are
connected. Besides, the thief would have to be
fast, as the other thefts have taken place in
separate areas of Moreland, hundreds of miles
apart." Watson pointed to several places on the
map far apart from each other as he flew. "It
just doesn't make any sense."

"I know, but ..." Grace trailed off. There
was something tugging at her brain about the
thefts, but she wasn't sure what. "I'd better do
the report and move on." Grace flipped open

the digi-screen beside the map, typed *Stolen spanner, puffin* into the mission-report section and pressed save.

"Lazy," Watson said with a tut, landing beside Grace again. "You finished that report faster than I could blink."

"I'm keeping it simple," said Grace, raising her eyebrows. "This is my fifth report in three days. No one has time to read them anyway."

Just as she said this, Grace's mother breezed into the map room towel-drying her hair. "Honestly, I don't think I'm going to get the stink of Rotty Marsh out of my hair," Ann Griffin said. "It wasn't my favourite day at work to rescue five robotic carts and horses that were neck deep in mud during a storm." She glanced at Grace and narrowed her eyes. "You *are* filling in your reports properly, aren't you?"

"Of course," Grace said, smiling at her mum. She flashed Watson a "don't you dare" look as he moved to open his beak. Grace's stomach groaned and she noticed it was past teatime. "What's for tea, Mum?"

"Er ... Is it that time already?" Ann said. "I haven't had a moment to think." She looked at the digi-screen beside the map and sighed. "We've had thirty calls in one week – our busiest time ever. Is Bren still on a mission?"

Grace looked down at the notepad beside the map and nodded. Bren had written *Gone to emergency in Floom.* Her stomach grumbled loudly again. "About tea?"

"Watson, you couldn't rustle up one of your vegetable stews, could—" Ann began, but stopped as two gates began flashing on the map almost at the same time – one red and the other blue. "Darn it, I thought that would be it for the day." Ann sighed. "Do you mind taking the blue call, Grace? I'll take the red and we'll meet back here for dinner. Watson, you go with Grace and see if you can pick up a pizza – there's a nice place in Grimble, where the blue call is coming from."

Ann kissed Grace on the head, passed her an apple from the fruit dish and grabbed a re-compass. She scribbled her destination on the notepad, then reached towards the flashing red gate. Ann Griffin disappeared into the map with a whirl and a flash of blue.

Grace stuffed her own re-compass into one of the many pockets of her uniform jumpsuit, then tapped her shoulder and Watson flew to it. "Come on, let's see what's up in Grimble," Grace said. "Most importantly ..." She picked up a pen then, tummy rumbling, she wrote: *Gone to Grimble to help and for PIZZA.*

Grimble wasn't the prettiest town in Moreland. The buildings were straight and square, and the smoke that rose from several factories seemed to hang in the air, giving it a dusty grey gloom.

The cobbles beside the old red box that had been used to call the wardens were wet with drizzle. Great Grandma Griffin had copied these boxes from olden times, when they had contained something called a telephone – now they were used by the people of Moreland to call the wardens when they needed help. A woman in blue overalls with short chestnut hair stood beside the box and beckoned to Grace.

The woman pulled Grace under her umbrella and smiled. "Thank you for coming so fast. I'm from Olive's Oils. I'm Olive." She pointed at a shop. It happened to be next to the pizza parlour, which wafted out a delicious smell.

Grace knew of Olive's Marvellous Machine Oil – it was the finest oil in Moreland and perfect for oiling Watson's joints. "I'm Warden Grace Griffin," she told Olive. "How can I help you?"

Olive ushered her into the shop, where row upon row of oils were stacked. "I don't like to bother you about such a small matter, but this is the third time it's happened this month."

She pointed to a shelf of neatly placed tins, where a single one was missing. "You see, I re-stock the oil before I leave every evening," Olive explained. "The shelves are always neat and full for the next day. This evening I shut the shop and went out the back – when I heard a noise. I came inside again, but there was no one here, yet a tin of oil had gone."

Grace took out her notepad and wrote *Stolen oil*. "There was definitely no sign of anyone?" she asked.

Olive shrugged. "No. I've told the Lawmakers, but they're as confused as me. I thought you wardens might be able to help, since you have such a great track record."

"Do you mind if I look around?" Grace asked.

"Please do."

Grace checked for fingerprints using the special powder and brush from one of her pockets, but there weren't any. There were also no signs of anyone forcing their way inside.

"There's nothing, Watson, just like Carp Cove," Grace whispered. "I hate to admit it, but I'm puzzled by all of these strange thefts."

"Indeed," Watson agreed. "It's hard to put facts together when there aren't many!"

Grace's stomach groaned. "Well, it's a fact that my belly is empty and there's a pizza parlour next door." She winked at Watson, then stood up and looked over to Olive at the counter. "I'm afraid the thief hasn't left any evidence at all, so I'll fit a second door lock for you as extra security and let you know if I get any leads."

"Right you are, thank you for looking," said Olive.

Grace and Watson fitted the second lock in no time. "All done," Grace said. "Do give us another call if it happens again." She waved goodbye, then noticed one of Watson's feathers lying by the door. "Here, Watson, we'll need to reconnect this when we get home."

Watson lifted his head back. "That's not one of mine," he said. "My feathers are much sleeker!"

Grace stared at the feather more closely and realised he was right. "Oh. Then what's a feather doing in the shop?" Grace called back to Olive, "You don't own any pet birds, do you?"

"Birds?" Olive said. "Not me, deary."

Grace shrugged and put the feather in one of her jumpsuit pockets. She had a feeling that something about it was plain odd.

2

Carp Cove

The following day, Ann Griffin took the first call, and Bren and Grace decided to fit in some training. Mum said it was important to keep fit and be able to defend yourself. Most of the calls they got were resolved without any trouble, but you never knew what to expect.

Grace and Bren faced each other on the training mat in the corner of the map room in Griffin House. They bowed.

"Have you still not solved any of the thefts?" asked Bren.

"I'm working on them," Grace replied as she took a pace towards him.

Bren stepped to the right, his hands ready to lunge. "Really?"

"And I expect you would have solved them all by now?" Grace said, and moved to circle with Bren. She didn't take her eyes from his but looked from the corner of her vision for a weakness to attack.

Bren shrugged. "I'm too busy rescuing people from floods and searching for missing pets down wells to worry about the odd loaf of bread and tin of oil going missing!"

As Bren lifted a leg to step forwards, Grace lunged and swept his other leg from beneath him, but as he fell he managed to grab her. They both ended up in a tangled mess on the mat.

"One point to me," said Grace.

"That was not a point." Bren tutted.
"Anyway, you only caught me off guard because
I'm tired."

"Excuses, excuses," Grace said.

Watson coughed. "When you two have finished, there's a blue call coming in."

Bren looked over. "Could you take it, Grace?" he asked. "I've only had a couple of hours' sleep."

"Sure. Oh, I forgot to tell you, there's cold pizza in the fridge."

"Yum, my kind of breakfast," Bren said. "Don't tell Mum, Watson."

"A healthy breakfast will keep your mind sharp," Watson said in Mum's voice.

"Come on, you," Grace said to Watson as she went to the map and he flew to her shoulder. "It's Jackville. Wasn't I there last week?" She shrugged, scribbled on the notepad, grabbed a re-compass, then teleported into the map with Watson.

Jackville was a small town in the north that Grace knew because there was a shop there that sold excellent tools. Mum had taken her there on business a few times. The call Grace had answered in Jackville last week had come from Betty Green, the owner of the tool shop.

Today Grace and Watson teleported to one end of a stone bridge, directly beside the red call box. Jackville had a cosy yet modern feel to it, with clean white buildings mixed with stone. A tram-trax mechanical transport cart rumbled by underneath the bridge, and the feet of the tall metal street lamps clattered on the road. The town was famous for these walking street lamps, which followed people around when it was dark, lighting their way.

Betty Green was waiting for Grace outside her shop – Grace recognised her unruly silver curls and denim dungarees. "I'm sorry to bother you again, Warden Griffin," Betty said, "but there's been another theft. This time I saw something. You won't believe it, but I was crouched behind the desk tidying up when a bird sneaked in and took a roll of wire!"

This week was getting stranger by the minute. Grace narrowed her eyes. "How odd. What would a bird want with a roll of wire?" she said, thinking out loud.

With a shrug, Betty Green said, "It's weird, I realise, but I know what I saw."

Grace took out her notepad. "Oh, I believe you," she said. She couldn't help but remember Mr Minnow being sure that a bird had stolen his jar of jam. *And* there was the recent mention of a puffin, along with the feather in Olive's shop. Was there some kind of pattern unfolding with birds and thefts?

"Can you describe the bird for me?" Grace asked.

"It was shorter than my knee, with black and white feathers," said Betty.

"A magpie?" Grace suggested. There were several magpies nesting near Griffin House in Copperport. They'd been known to take shiny things.

"No, larger than that," Betty said. "It had triangle eyes on a white face, a bit like a clown, and a big orange beak. It was more like one of those birds you see at the seaside."

Once again the theft from Carp Cove popped into Grace's head. "Was it a puffin by any chance?" she asked.

"That's the one," Betty said with a laugh. "Strange, right?"

Grace remembered the feather in her pocket from the shop in Grimble. She pulled it out and had another look. She turned to Watson on her shoulder. "It could be a puffin tail feather," Grace said.

Watson thought for a moment and nodded.

"Well, I think I've got all I need for now," Grace told Betty. "I'll be back in touch."

Back at Griffin House in Copperport, Grace packed a rucksack with food and other useful items – including a rope and a sheet of canvas to sit on or make a tent with. "Mum, I'm going back to Carp Cove," Grace said.

"Really? Why?" Ann Griffin asked with a yawn. She hadn't got back from a call until late the night before.

"I'm still looking into the small thefts," Grace said. "I think they may be connected, but I need more proof."

Ann Griffin nodded and closed her eyes in the chair. Grace knew that her mum was exhausted due to all the calls that had been coming in recently. It was good that Grace and Bren were able to help with missions, but it wasn't enough. They were all rushed off their feet and there didn't seem to be any sign of things calming down.

Grace and Bren had suggested to their mum several times that they should find someone else they could train to help them. Ann refused to even discuss it, but Grace thought this might be a good time to try again.

"Mum, you're so tired," she said. "Don't you think it's time that we tried to get some—"

Ann interrupted her. "I know what you're going to say and I'm fine, Grace. I'm just resting

my eyes. Remember Great Grandma Griffin's
map rule number ten: keep it in the family.
We're OK as we are."

"But times have changed," Grace argued.
"There are a lot more people in Moreland than
when Great Grandma Griffin was alive. I bet
she didn't have anywhere near as many calls.

Couldn't we perhaps advertise for someone to help?" Grace thought it might be fun to have another warden around the place.

"Stop it, Grace," Ann said. "The map is a very important piece of technology and we can't risk it being used by anyone outside the family. I don't trust anyone but you and Bren. Now make sure you take a re-compass, a digi-com and Watson."

The salty seaside village of Carp Cove looked as if it had been forgotten by time. Not more than ten crooked buildings in bright colours were bunched on the beach of the small bay. White cliffs edged the cove, dazzling in the midday sun, and the sapphire sea glistened below. A few small boats bobbed happily near the shore. Out at sea, Grace could make out an island with a twisted old building perched on it.

"Eely Isle," said a voice from close by. "That was a fine castle not long ago."

"Mr Minnow!" Grace called, recognising the voice. The old man was inside one of the small boats resting on the beach. She hurried over. "What are you doing?"

"Having a lunchtime nap, of course," Mr Minnow said. "It's Warden Grace Griffin, isn't it? Did I put in a call?" He glanced towards the red box, taking off his fisherman's cap and scratching his bald head. Mr Minnow had a lot of thick white hair on his upper lip and chin but not a whisker on his head.

"Not this time, Mr Minnow," said Grace. "I decided to come back and see if I can get to the bottom of your missing items."

"Call me Fergus, lass," Mr Minnow told Grace. "You must be a mind-reader, because I lost a tin of baked beans yesterday, but I didn't want to bother you by calling again. It's most likely I misplaced them, eh?"

"Did you see anything?" Grace asked.

"You'll think I'm daft, but I'm sure I saw a puffin by the shop again," Fergus Minnow said. "There are hundreds of them nesting up on the cliff, of course, but they're shy and would never normally venture into town."

Grace looked to the cliffs and could make out some black and white specks. "Do they tend to like beans?" she asked doubtfully.

Fergus Minnow chuckled. "They go wild for fish like herring and hake, but not normally baked beans."

Grace gazed out to sea for a moment, wondering if the ocean lacked fish for some reason, leading the puffins to come down to the village to steal food. It seemed unlikely. "So there's not a shortage of fish?" she asked.

27

"Not as far as I know," Fergus said.

"Would you mind if I hang around for a while, Fergus? I'd really like to get to the bottom of this."

"Be my guest, lass."

3

Stake Out

Grace and Watson found a spot behind a fishing hut where they could see the entrance to Mr Minnow's shop. Over the next hour or so, a few villagers came and went for supplies of milk and loaves of bread, but nothing strange happened. Eventually, the sun began to set, lighting up the shop windows in a peachy blaze.

Grace took out the small picnic she'd packed and began nibbling away. She watched Mr Minnow flip the sign on the shop door to "Closed", and then he tottered up the cobbles towards his small white fishing cottage.

"Doesn't look like we're going to see any action today, Watson," said Grace, stuffing a jam tart in her mouth.

"Sadly, I agree," Watson said. "You fitting a whole jam tart in your mouth is probably the most unusual thing to happen in Carp Cove today."

Grace nudged his wing and swallowed. "You're just jealous you can't eat. Perhaps we should wait another hour, then head back."

Watson nodded.

Sunset turned to dusk and the warm glow of lights from the cottages made Grace long for the cosy fire at Griffin House. She yawned, saying, "Let's call it a day."

But as she stood up and brushed herself down, a movement on the path caught her eye. A small shape slipped between the shadows towards the row of shops. At first, Grace thought she was seeing things, as it was far too small to be a person.

"Watson, are you seeing what I am?" she whispered.

"Switching to night vision," Watson said. Something behind his eyes whirred as he tracked the small shape bobbing towards Mr Minnow's shop. "Well, it seems as if Betty Green and Mr Minnow were right. That looks like a puffin to me."

They watched, transfixed, as the puffin neared the door to the shop, rapidly fluttered its wings and rose up to the door handle. Then the door swung inwards and the puffin disappeared inside.

"Should we go after it?" asked Watson.

"No," Grace said. "If it sees us, it'll be startled and we might lose it. We don't want to simply catch the puffin in the act of stealing –

we want to see where it's come from. If we can follow it back to its nest, perhaps we'll find evidence of the other missing items."

After less than thirty seconds, the puffin reappeared at the door.

Watson's eyes whirred again. "Grace, it seems to be clutching a loaf of bread under its wing."

"I've heard puffins were clever, but this is incredible," said Grace. "The way it opened the door, I mean. Birds don't go around opening doors – apart from you, of course, Watson. Come on, let's follow it."

Silently, they scurried up the path behind the bird. The puffin's white cheeks and belly shone in the moonlight.

Eventually the puffin stopped a short distance from the cliff edge. In the twilight, Grace could see many other puffins dotted around the clifftop. Several disappeared into dark holes in the grass.

"Keep an eye on our puffin, Watson," whispered Grace. "Look, it's going towards that burrow."

The puffin stopped and looked around slowly as it reached the hole in the ground.

Grace and Watson dived behind a large clump of earth.

The cogs in Watson's head ticked softly as he asked, "What's it doing?"

"Seeing if it's being followed by the look of it."

The burrow in front of the puffin was wider than the others – Grace guessed this was so it could store everything it'd been taking. She watched as the puffin took a springy jump and dived straight in to the burrow.

"It's cornered now, Watson," Grace said. "Come on." They hurried over and stopped at the entrance to the burrow. "Maybe you should go first, Watson, and see how big it is inside. You're smaller and I think I'll only just fit."

Watson hesitated. "Have puffins been known to attack ravens?" he asked.

"Don't be silly," Grace said, pushing him forwards. "You're bigger than it *and* trained in combat."

Watson hopped around the edge, then jumped inside.

Grace peered in after him and a flash of orange light blinded her. "Watson, are you all right?" she called, worrying he'd been attacked by a stun stick. "Watson?" she yelled more urgently, but there was no reply.

Grace dropped to her knees and tried to see further inside the burrow. It was as black as outer space. Then Grace saw a shimmer in the dark, as if an invisible curtain flickered in a breeze. "Watson," she tried again. "Are you hurt?"

She fumbled in her pocket for a torch, switched it on and shone it into the gloom.

The burrow opened up to a large empty hole. There was no sign of the puffin or Watson, so Grace thought there must be a passage leading off somewhere.

The torchlight bounced off the earthy walls. Grace's chest tightened with panic. Then she saw the strange flicker again. She leaned further in to take a look, and her knees slipped, sending her tumbling inside.

For a moment, Grace fell through the darkness, then there was a flash of orange light. Her stomach lurched with sickness and her body felt as if it was being sucked into the small neck of a bottle until she rolled onto a patch of earth.

4

Eely Isle

At first Grace just stared up at the stars above, blinking and groaning as she tried to keep down the jam tart she'd eaten earlier. She was lying among roots and damp grass. But how could she be back outside when she'd just fallen into a burrow?

Grace suspected she knew the answer. She had teleported. There was no mistaking the sensation she'd had in the burrow. But how had it happened? It certainly wasn't as smooth as teleporting through the gates on the Griffin map.

She sat up, took her torch from her pocket and looked around. She was nowhere near a red call box and she definitely wasn't back in the map room of Griffin House. Behind her was a large tree with a hole in the base from which she must have tumbled. Somewhere close by she could hear the wash of waves, as if she was near the sea.

Grace tried to make sense of what was happening and became aware of a curious ticking noise. She turned around to see where it was coming from and found a puffin staring at her. It held a loaf of bread under its wing.

As Grace stared at the puffin, Watson flew from a nearby branch and landed on her lap. "About time you showed up," he said.

"Where are we and what is going on?" Grace asked him.

"I've no idea."

Grace stared at the puffin, then finally said, "Hello?" She felt a bit daft, trying to talk to a puffin, but this was clearly no ordinary bird.

The puffin leaned closer and Grace heard the soft ticking again. "Watson, it's like you!" she realised. "It's a robot puffin!"

"It's far inferior," Watson scoffed. "It doesn't seem to talk for one thing."

"It might seem inferior, but it's using some sort of portal," Grace said. "I thought the portals on the Griffin map and the re-compass were the only ways to teleport …"

Grace's voice trailed off as she searched her brain for answers. She frowned, then looked around, trying to work out where they were. There were a few trees, some patches of thick grass and a strong salty wind.

"Perhaps we're still near Carp Cove," Grace said. She narrowed her eyes, trying to make out a large dark shape a short distance away. Milky moonlight lit the edges of a jagged building that looked a bit like a ... "Castle!" Grace said, thinking back to Carp Cove and the island out at sea. She remembered Mr Minnow calling it Eely Isle and saying that there was a castle on it. Could that be where they were?

A faint yellow glow was coming from a window in one of the walls. "Come on, Watson," Grace said. "I think someone might live here. Let's investigate."

Watson cleared his throat. "Perhaps we should just go home and tell your mum what we've found."

"Let's try to figure it out for ourselves. Mum and Bren are already so busy."

"Well, at least let your mum know what we're doing," said Watson.

Grace sighed. "All right. I'll send a message now with the digi-com." This was a new piece of technology Ann Griffin had invented so the Griffins could contact each other wherever they were in Moreland.

Grace took the palm-sized white disc from her pocket and clicked the neon yellow circle in the middle. Ann Griffin's voice said, "I'm out on a call, please leave a message."

Grace spoke into the device. "Mum, I'm still in Carp Cove, sort of, and I think we're getting somewhere. Me and Watson are both fine and we have supplies to stay overnight if we need to. I'll check in again soon." She looked to Watson and asked, "Satisfied?"

Watson gave a nod. "I suppose a quick look at the building won't do any harm. What about the puffin?"

Grace scanned the dark. "Where's it gone?"

"It must've slipped away while we were talking," Watson said. "I thought you were watching it."

Grace frowned. "And I thought you were," she told Watson. "Come on, let's head towards the castle and see if we can find it."

They clambered across the grass towards the castle. As they got closer, it was clear that the building was in a worse state than Grace had thought. It looked as if several walls had collapsed and chunks of rock were strewn all around. "It's in ruins," Grace said.

Watson raised his wing and pointed to a window above. "But what's making the light?"

Slowly, they approached the glowing window. Grace turned off her torch and stood on a piece of fallen rock to look inside. To her great surprise, a boy around her age sat on the floor of the room leaning over a candle reading a book. The room was simply furnished with a few worn but cosy-looking armchairs and a coffee table with a fringed tablecloth.

"Oh, look at that," Grace whispered to Watson, then she lost her footing and slipped off the rock with a loud, "Argh!"

Seconds later, the window above creaked open.

A boy with messy blond hair peered out. He held a candle, but a gust of wind blew it out. "Who's there?" he called, his voice trembling.

Grace fumbled in her pocket for her torch as she said, "My name's Grace Griffin."

She switched on the torch and shone the light upwards at the boy's face. He winced.

"Oh, I'm sorry!" Grace said, then turned the light and shone it under her own chin.

He jumped back, alarmed.

"I realise that probably made me look scary, but I'm just a girl," Grace said. She smiled and stood up. "I didn't mean to frighten you."

"What are you doing here?" the boy asked. "Are you alone?" He looked around warily.

"Yes, just me," Grace replied.

Watson coughed.

"And a robot raven," she added.

"Did you come by boat?" the boy asked.

"Not exactly."

"By which she means not at all," added Watson.

The boy glared at them, clearly confused.

"What's your name?" asked Grace.

"Tom Eely."

"Then this *is* Eely Isle?" she asked, excited. She lowered her voice and added, "Sorry, I don't want to wake your family."

Tom looked backwards. "Yes, they're in bed. I was just up late working on something."

"I don't mean to disturb you," said Grace, "but I wonder if I can ask you a couple of questions?"

"OK."

"This may sound odd, but ... have you ever seen a puffin or a portal on the island?"

"A what?" Tom asked.

"A puffin or a portal."

"I thought that's what you said." Tom frowned. "There are puffins on the cliffs of Carp Cove."

"But not on this island?" Grace asked.

Tom shook his head. His face was round, but his cheekbones were sharp and thin. His eyes were as blue as the sea on a sunny day but with a sad feeling to them.

"And no portal that you know of?" Grace said. "They're special gateways that transport you from one place to another."

Tom looked at Grace as if she was mad, then said, "No, there are no portals on the island that I know of. What's your uniform? You're a bit young to be a Lawmaker."

Grace brushed herself down. "I'm a warden from Copperport," she explained.

"Look, can you just go back to wherever you came from?" Tom said. "It's night-time and my family don't like people snooping around the island."

Grace smiled and nodded. "Just keep an eye on your belongings. There are some troublesome puffins stealing things in these parts."

Tom gave a nervous laugh of disbelief and shut the window.

"Well, he thinks we're completely bonkers," said Watson as they made their way back towards the portal tree.

Grace shrugged. Nothing made sense.

When they arrived back at the tree, there was still no sign of the puffin and all was quiet. "I'll be glad to get home," yawned Watson.

"Robots don't need to yawn," Grace said, frowning.

"Sadly some human habits are wired into my programming," Watson replied. "It's meant to make me likeable."

"Well, we're not going home yet."

"Grace, it must be almost midnight!"

"We'll send Mum another message to say we're camping out," Grace said. "I bet that puffin is trying to steal something from the Eely family now, so we're going to wait here until it's back, then follow it until we find out who is behind this. And if the puffin doesn't come back, then we'll look for clues in the daylight."

"I don't suppose I can change your mind in favour of a comfy warm bed?" Watson asked.

Grace took out the feather she'd found at Olive's Oils and tickled Watson under the chin. "Don't be such a softy, Watson. It'll be fun – plus, the weirder this mystery gets, the more determined I am to solve it."

5

Tom Eely

Grace and Watson collected some kindling and wood to make a fire near the portal tree. Grace was glad to be wearing her warden's jumpsuit with its many pockets and tools. She had the fire lit in no time at all with the help of her flint striker, and she made a hammock using her canvas and rope.

Grace thought that the robot puffin might come back in the night, so Watson offered to keep watch as he didn't need to sleep. But by morning there was still no sign of it.

Luckily Grace had packed plenty of snacks in her rucksack, even if they were a bit random. She didn't mind a breakfast of marshmallows, peanut butter sandwiches and strawberry laces, with some blackberries that she'd found growing nearby.

Grace left another message for Mum on the digi-com, then packed up her things. In the daylight, a trail of three-pronged puffin footprints could be seen in the mud, heading away from the tree.

"Look, Watson, if we follow the footprints, we might be able to find some more clues," Grace said.

"Yes, there seem to be enough prints to track."

They soon emerged from the group of trees and followed the footprints up a slope, and the island landscape came more clearly into view. Across the sea, the mainland stretched from north to south, with the beach and village of Carp Cove just visible across from the island.

Eely Isle itself was rugged, with patchy grassland, rocky mounds and clumps of trees. In the centre of the island was the castle, which looked in an even worse state in the daylight. Parts of the building were in total ruins or looked as if they might tumble down at any moment.

The area where she'd met Tom Eely the night before was the mid-section and the only part that looked liveable. Towards the back Grace could see a central turret, the highest point, which also looked in one piece.

Grace and Watson tracked the puffin prints. They disappeared where the mud turned to grass, but it was still possible to see a trail trodden across the meadow. It led in the direction of the castle.

As they got closer, Watson flew down to land, blocking Grace's path. "Perhaps we should knock at the castle before we start snooping around," Watson said. "You did rather startle that poor boy last night."

"Yes, probably," Grace agreed. "But it all seems very quiet." She pointed to a gap in the castle wall. "It looks like the puffin went in via this hole."

She bent and peered inside. The room beyond had a broken bed lit by a stream of light from a hole in the roof. A tattered mound of fabric was stacked on the floor along with a few cups and plates. "If the puffin was trying to steal from here," Grace said, "it doesn't seem like there's much to take."

Watson coughed as if to get her attention.

"Whatever is it?" Grace turned to see the boy from the night before standing a few metres away and frowning. "Oh, Tom. Hello."

Her cheeks filled with warmth at being caught peering into the boy's home. "Watson, perhaps fly up and see if you can spot the puffin."

"There are better rooms in the main wing," said Tom.

"I'm sorry, I wasn't snooping," Grace said.

"Really?" Tom said crossly. "Because it kind of looks like you are."

"Perhaps a little." Grace stood up and punched Tom playfully on the arm. "We followed the puffin's footprints. It must have come here last night. Have you noticed anything missing?" She looked down at Tom's frayed cuffs and noticed his jumper had a hole in the belly.

"There's no need for fancy clothes on the island," Tom said, spotting her glance. "And no, there's nothing missing."

"I didn't mean to stare," Grace said. "I was just thinking I like the red of your jumper. It's like raspberries." She looked up at the castle. "Do you mind if I speak to your parents?

Perhaps they've noticed missing items or discovered the portal."

"I'm afraid they ... went fishing early this morning."

Frowning, Grace looked out to sea. She didn't want to leave the island until she had at least one new clue or piece of evidence. "Perhaps I could wait for them," Grace said.

Tom looked down and frowned again. "They really don't like visitors just turning up on the island."

"Then they will be very interested to learn that a puffin thief has targeted them," Grace said with a nod of satisfaction. "I'll stay out of your way until they're back and just have a look around. Unless ..." Grace trailed off, thinking. She had been so busy being a warden lately that she missed hanging out with friends, and this boy seemed a little lonely. "You could show me around a bit?"

Watson flew back and landed on her shoulder. "No sign of the puffin," he said. "Maybe it slipped past us back into the portal last night. Perhaps when I rested my batteries for a minute."

"Or it might still be here somewhere?" Grace said, raising her eyebrows.

"I think I'd know if there was a thieving puffin on the island," said Tom defensively.

Grace brushed down her uniform. "If there's one thing I've learned so far as a warden, it's that criminals can be crafty. Even puffins." She smiled at Tom. "So how about that tour?"

He shuffled his feet for a moment. Grace wondered if he went to school on the mainland and if he ever had friends come and visit him here.

"Maybe just a quick tour," Tom said, his face brightening. Grace thought he must be warming to having them on the island.

Tom led Grace around the edge of the castle. She noticed he was glancing at her nervously and realised she hadn't really explained who she was and what a warden did. So she told Tom about their map and why the puffin and the portal they'd discovered was so strange.

"So your great grandma invented the map technology?" Tom said.

"Yes, she did it when she was young and developed it during her life," Grace replied.

"It must be really cool to be part of such a great family."

Grace swelled with pride, as she really did think she was the luckiest person in the land. But she saw a sad look in Tom's eyes, so she just shrugged and said, "It's OK." He did seem a little lonely.

"But your parents must be really smart," Grace said, pointing to some clever stilts holding up part of the building, and a slide coming out of a hole in the wall.

"I did that, actually." Tom blushed.

"Wow, it's incredible," Grace said. She wondered if Mum would let her build a slide from her bedroom down to the map room at Griffin House.

"And this bit round here where the windows have broken, I've made some shutters," Tom said. "They collect energy from the sun and transform it into light and heat."

"Cool!" Grace said.

Tom seemed to smile more as he showed her around. "And over there," he went on, "I built a pulley swing to get from one section of the castle to the other."

"That looks fun. Can I have a go?" Grace asked.

"Would you like to?" Tom's face lit up, then he paused. "My parents will be back any moment. They really don't like strangers."

"But we're not strangers any more," Grace pointed out. "We've been talking for over an hour now."

Watson coughed. "We should go back to base and check in with your mum."

Grace frowned at Watson. She liked Tom, but something about the Eelys and the island wasn't as it seemed and she wanted to get to the bottom of it.

"We'll call in again on the digi-com," Grace said to Watson. Then she turned to Tom. "How about you show us a bit more, then we have some lunch?"

"It's a bit early for lunch," Tom said.

Grace tapped her bag. "It's never too early for peanut butter sandwiches and jam tarts."

6

Puffin Robots

As the day went on, there was still no sign of Tom's parents or the puffin. They stopped for lunch at a beach in the north of the island, then Tom took them back to the castle.

"My parents must have decided to go to the mainland for supplies." Tom shrugged.

"We can stay a bit longer," Grace said. "Perhaps we can wait at the jetty – we haven't been there yet."

Tom shook his head. "It's a bit boring there."

"Then could we have a look inside the castle?" Grace asked. She was getting impatient and more suspicious about his parents being away for so long. Then again, her mum was often away for hours at a time on missions.

"Perhaps just my room," Tom said. "My parents don't like—"

"Snooping. I remember." Grace smiled.

They walked into the stony entrance and Grace whispered to Watson, "Keep him talking when I say I'm going to call Mum."

Tom unbolted the front door and Grace and Watson followed him inside. They walked up a narrow hallway and went into Tom's room. It was full of tools and gadgets: spanners, wheels, wrenches, plates of metal and so on.

"It looks like you keep yourself busy," Grace said.

"It's fun making things," Tom replied. "I'm working on an alarm so that I can detect intruders."

Grace laughed. "That's a good idea with that thieving puffin around."

"Or wardens who teleport onto your island," Watson said quietly to Grace. Then he flew over to Tom. "Show me how the alarm works? I might be able to help. I've set up an excellent alarm system back at Griffin House."

As Tom began to explain, Grace said she needed to call home and slipped out into the hallway. But instead of taking out her digi-com, she hurried along the strange curved hall and found herself in an open courtyard. There were many arched doorways around the sides and a path led to the tall tower she'd spotted earlier. But where should she explore? There wasn't much time before Tom would become suspicious.

Then Grace noticed small muddy puffin footprints heading towards one of the arched doorways. She used her pocket torch to light the way and followed the prints down a stony staircase. Perhaps it would lead to another portal? Maybe there was a network of portals, and if she followed them they would take her to the mastermind thief.

At the bottom of the steps Grace stopped dead. She was facing a large stone-walled workshop filled with wires and oddments of machines and computer equipment. Many sets of eyes stared back at her.

The room was full of puffins. They were all in different states of repair: fully made, half made, robot parts. She thought she'd been following one puffin, but there were many, and they were being made here.

Grace wasn't surprised Tom's parents didn't like people snooping around: *they* were making the robot thieves. Perhaps there were so many

puffins because they were planning bigger thefts. And poor Tom seemed unaware of all of it.

Somewhere in the distance, a voice called Grace's name. As fast as a spark, she ran back up the stairs to the courtyard. Just as she did, Tom shouted from the hallway.

Grace dashed towards him. "Sorry, I couldn't get a signal, so I went a bit further along the hall. Anyway, I think we've imposed for too long. Come on, Watson, we should go home."

Watson narrowed his eyes. Grace knew he would be suspicious about her giving up so easily.

"Mum said it's turning into another busy day," Grace went on, "and Bren needs a break, so we should head back. Mum said some mysteries can't be solved and to leave this one."

Tom looked half relieved that they were going and half sad.

"We'll head back for one last look at the portal, then use the re-compass," Grace said. "I don't fancy travelling through that portal again if I can help it. It made me feel rather sick!"

Tom stood at the main castle door, watching them walk towards the woods. As soon as they were out of sight, Grace stopped.

"You didn't call home, did you?" said Watson.

"I didn't have time," Grace said. "I found a room full of robot puffins! It's the Eelys. They're making them!"

Watson ruffled his feathers. "I knew something wasn't right."

"And I had another thought. Maybe sending out single robot puffins is just the start.

Perhaps all the small thefts are test runs for a bigger robbery!"

"It does seem strange just to steal small things," Watson agreed. "You could be right. We should call in and alert your mum."

Grace nodded. "There's one more thing I want to check first."

7

Signs

Grace and Watson kept out of sight of the castle as they climbed down the rocky slope to the beach, then across the pebbles towards the jetty.

"I want to see if I can spot a boat returning to the island," Grace said. "The Eelys can't possibly be much longer, even if they went to the mainland for supplies." Her heart leapt as she saw a boat tied to the jetty. "They must be back!" she gasped. "But how did we miss them? Watson, take a quick flight and check they're not walking back to the castle."

Watson made a swift loop above, then landed on the jetty and confirmed there was no sign of Tom's family.

"They can't just vanish," Grace said. Everything about this island puzzled her. But that just made her more determined to solve the mystery. "Let's take a closer look at the boat."

It was a medium-sized boat that must have looked magnificent in its best condition, but now the boat's white paint was chipped and a faded strip of sky blue wrapped around the hull. There were two masts with their sails folded, although Grace could see a large rip in one. A tarnished brass bell was attached to the bow.

Grace stepped inside the boat, took out her notepad and wrote: *Fishing net, rods, empty jugs, rusty can – all DRY.*

She turned to Watson. "Perhaps they did go for supplies. It doesn't look as if they've been fishing."

Watson nodded. "My thoughts exactly."

Like lightning, a new thought struck Grace. What if Tom's parents had gone and he was here alone? She shook her head: it was highly unlikely.

LY OR HAN GE

Grace jumped back onto the jetty and turned to study the boat again. She noted a name painted on the side:

LY OR HAN GE

"What a strange name for a boat," Grace said.

"What's an or-han-ge?" Watson frowned.

Grace's diqi-com vibrated and flashed in her pocket. She took it out and pressed the button.

"Grace, are you there?" the voice said. It was Bren.

"Sorry," Grace replied. "I meant to check in. It's just that things have been getting stranger here."

"Mum's just left for a call," Bren told Grace. "A large robbery. She said to tell you she's put a block on blue calls on the map until you get back. She said if you can't solve your case in the next hour, to forget it and move on to a new mission."

"I'll be back soon," Grace said. "I promise." She clicked the button to end the call.

"Perhaps we should just go," said Watson.

"No way. If Tom's parents *are* back and Mum's been called to a robbery, then perhaps the two—"

"Grace, two and three do not make four," Watson interrupted.

She frowned. "Watson, I know that. Don't be annoying."

He rolled his eyes and Grace marched back up the jetty with new determination. "Come on. Tom's hiding something from us and I'm going to find out what it is."

8

Suspicion

Grace clambered up a grassy hill in the direction of the castle.

"Ow!" she yelped. In her hurry, she'd caught her hand on something in the grass. Probably a nettle. She examined her finger and pulled out a splinter of wood.

Grace looked down to see something brown and wooden buried in the overgrowth. A few letters were visible – it seemed to be an old sign which had fallen down. She ripped away at the grass, finally pulling it out. "Watson, hold that side." He extended his wing and Grace stood back and read:

EE   O PHA AGE

She thought back to the name of the boat: LY OR HAN GE. Then she opened her mouth wide and smiled. "Watson, they're the same. They're just missing different letters! If we put them together ..." But it was hard for Grace's mind to join the two. "Eely is the first word, right?"

The cogs of Watson's brain whirred, then he declared, "The second is orphanage. They both read Eely Orphanage!"

"How curious," Grace said. "There's no orphanage here. Only Tom's tumbledown family castle." Grace pushed up her jumpsuit sleeves. "Right: petty thefts, robot puffins, a crumbling castle, missing parents and now a non-existent orphanage. It's time to get to the bottom of this once and for all."

Grace stomped back towards the castle and up the front steps. It was now late afternoon and soon it'd be sunset. As Grace approached, she noticed figures beyond one of the windows. Tom's parents must be home! How had she missed them coming back from their boat? Perhaps they'd used the portal ...

She gestured to Watson to be silent and sneaked beneath the broken window, where a tatty white curtain wafted in the breeze. Grace watched the figures move oddly from side to side. They had an almost floaty walk.

She decided to peek inside and reached to pull back the curtain.

The figures weren't real people. They were robots. A robot family! And Tom sat in the middle of them holding a control panel. Grace couldn't help but let out a gasp, and Tom looked over to the window.

"What are you doing?" he said, cheeks turning beetroot red.

"We didn't go home," Grace said, feeling guilty.

"Go away!" Tom shouted suddenly, and Grace jumped back from the window.

"Should we?" asked Watson nervously. "He looks pretty cross."

"No way," said Grace. She hurried up the steps and hammered on the castle door. "I'm not going until you let me in, Tom!"

After a short while, the bolt was pulled back and the door opened.

"I'm a warden of Copperport and I'm here to help," Grace said with determination. She thought how very skinny Tom looked in his thin T-shirt without his big woolly jumper. She softened her voice. "You live here by yourself, don't you? Tell me the truth, Tom."

He stared at a spot on the floor as if it might help him find the right words. Then Tom took a deep breath and looked at Grace. He pushed his scraggly blond hair behind his ears and said, "All right, I *am* alone. There are no parents, and I know all about the portal and the puffin." Tom's lip trembled and his cheeks seemed to turn even more ruby red. "Are you happy now?" he shouted.

9

The Orphanage

There was one secret tool that the Griffin
wardens kept in their uniform pockets. A tool
that helped when people were scared or angry,
even if it was rather unexpected. She'd seen
her mum use it many times.

Grace reached into the lower leg pocket of
her jumpsuit and pulled out a bag of jelly babies.
She unfolded the open bag and offered one to
Tom. "If you have something you'd like to share,
I'm a good listener," Grace said. "And so is
Watson." Then she added in a whisper, "Because

I can switch Watson to mute mode. This robot raven doesn't stop talking!"

"Hey! Cheeky," said Watson, ruffling his feathers.

Grace laughed. "Only joking, my robo friend."

Tom gave a smile and Grace knew it was working. He took a jelly baby and popped it in his mouth. His grin widened. "I haven't had anything like this in ages," Tom said. "You see, I only steal what I really need and even then I hate doing it, but ..."

Grace sat on the top step and patted the space beside her. "Why don't you start at the beginning?"

Tom sat next to her and after several long breaths, he began. "Eely Isle and the castle doesn't belong to my family. The castle was an orphanage. I grew up here because I was abandoned as a baby, left outside a shop in a village, and I was brought here."

"I'm sorry," said Grace, thinking of her own family and how much she would miss them if they weren't around.

"Oh, don't be sorry," Tom said. "It was the best thing that has ever happened to me. The orphanage was run by an amazing woman called Amy Eely." Tom paused, sadness dimming his blue eyes.

"She has the same last name as you," Grace said.

He nodded. "Because I was so young when I was abandoned, nobody knew my real name, so Amy gave me the name Tom and her last name, Eely. She was the kindest person and a brilliant scientist too. She didn't just look after all of the orphans here, she taught us engineering and mechanics, and encouraged us to be inventive. She always said that we may have had an unlucky start in life, but there was no reason to let it hold us back."

"So she was giving you the skills to go out into the world and do great things," Grace said.

Tom nodded. "That was what she always told us. And we had so much fun too. Hide and seek around the island, fishing together, trips to the mainland, invention competitions ..."

Grace could see that Tom was reliving the happy memories in his mind.

"She sounds amazing," said Grace. She wondered what had happened to Amy and the other children but knew Tom would tell her when he was ready.

"She was," Tom replied. "And Amy always said I had a flair for inventing and science, so she gave me extra lessons and let me help her with her secret projects."

Grace wondered if the secret project involved robot puffins and portals.

"But it was just Amy and us at the orphanage, no one else," Tom went on. "So when ..." He paused, his face muscles tight. "When she died suddenly, there was no one left to run the orphanage."

Grace passed him another jelly baby and Tom took it, then wiped away a tear with his tatty sleeve.

"All the orphans were taken to new homes on the mainland," Tom said

"What happened to you?" Grace asked.

"I didn't want to leave. So I hid."

It was clear how much Tom had loved Amy and how much the island meant to him.

"I locked some of the inventions away in the underground room and took the key so they couldn't get to them," Tom explained. "Then I hid in one of the trees until everyone had left. A few of the other orphans were planning to hide with me, but they were too scared in the end."

"That was a brave decision you made," Grace said. She knew if someone tried to make her leave Griffin House, she would do anything to stay. "Tell me about the portal. Did Amy invent it?"

He nodded. "We'd been working on the portals together before she died. She wanted to find a way for the children of the orphanage to come back and visit easily after they'd grown up and left. But we didn't get the portals working while she was alive."

"They're working now, if a bit clumsily." Grace held her stomach, remembering the

feeling of being squeezed into a bottle neck
when she had fallen into the portal.

"Over the past two years I've worked on
perfecting the portals," Tom said. "Amy left lots
of notes and I managed to fill in the gaps."

Watson and Grace raised their eyebrows
at each other – they were both impressed at

Tom's abilities. Great Grandma Griffin had been young when she'd developed the technology too.

"So Amy's been gone for two years?" Grace asked.

"Yes."

Yet the castle was in quite a mess in places. It seemed to Grace like Amy and the others had all been gone a lot longer.

Reading her thoughts, Tom said, "Some of my experiments damaged the castle. But it was worth it in the end when I got the portal working."

"And the puffin robots?"

"Amy used to make one for each orphan, just for fun," Tom said. "When I got the portal to work, it wasn't perfect and ready to teleport humans, so I sent the puffins. I could only survive for so long by fishing and foraging for berries, and the tinned food I'd locked away was running out. So I used the puffins to steal supplies." Tom's cheeks were red again. "I don't like doing it. I only take what I have to so I can survive and keep the inventions going."

Everything had fallen into place now. That was why Grace had had so many calls for small thefts of bread, oil and so on.

"Well, that's a lot to take in, Tom Eely, and it's made me rather hungry," Grace said. "Have you got any of that loaf left from Mr Minnow's shop? I have some jam in my rucksack and we could have jelly babies for pudding."

10

Mix-Up

Tom nipped away to get the bread. An idea fizzled inside Grace. "Watson, keep watch inside the hallway while I call Mum. Signal to me if Tom comes back before I finish."

Luckily Ann Griffin had just got back to Griffin House after a call, so Grace hurriedly told her mum about Tom. Grace was certain her idea could work.

"So he's been all alone on the island? Poor thing," said Mum.

"I know, but—" Grace started to say.

Mum carried on talking, "He probably thought it was a good idea at the time and now he's stuck."

"But, Mum, I—"

"Grace, it's our duty to tell the authorities. It's not right. Tom needs a home and they will be able to arrange that for him. It's lucky you found him so that we can help."

"Mum, listen, I—"

But the door creaked behind Grace and she turned to see Tom. He was holding Watson's beak closed, a look of shock on his face.

Grace quickly switched off the digi-com.

"I was starting to trust you," Tom said in a whisper.

"Tom, no, you don't understand," Grace protested.

"I told you everything and now you're just going to get me taken away!"

"But, Tom—"

He thrust a startled Watson into her hands. "Stay away from me and get off my island!"

"If you'll just listen!" Grace cried. But Tom ran back inside and bolted the door.

"That went well," said Watson.

"He didn't give me a chance to explain my idea," Grace said. "I was about to tell Mum all about Tom's incredible talents. How he's brilliant at inventing and how I think he would make a great warden."

"A warden?" Watson said. "Grace, are you thinking straight? You know we keep the wardens within the Griffin family."

"But that rule was made in the days of Great Grandma Griffin," Grace said. "When things weren't as busy. We have plenty of room at home and we're rushed off our feet. Tom would be brilliant. He's brave and smart and ..." She couldn't help thinking it would be so much fun to have someone her own age around Griffin House. A friend. She banged on the door and yelled, "Let us in, Tom! I need to explain. I won't let anyone take you, I promise."

But there was no answer.

"What shall we do?" asked Watson.

Grace had to find a way to speak to Tom and explain. "Luckily this castle is full of holes," she said. "We'll just have to find another way in."

11

Puffin Attack

Grace and Watson went searching for holes in the castle walls and windows, but it seemed they had been swiftly blocked by shutters.

"Tom must have had these shutters ready in case anyone ever came looking for him." Grace huffed, feeling frustrated.

The sun was setting behind the castle and a storm was brewing out to sea, casting an eerie bruised orange colour over everything.

"Watson, fly up and see if we can get in through one of the top windows," said Grace. "I have rope and a grappling hook. Find the best way up and in."

Watson took flight and circled the castle. He paused in the air for a moment before zooming down to land back in front of Grace.

"What's the matter?" she asked.

"It's Tom. He's on the roof of the tallest tower. He's got all the robot puffins up there with him, and ..."

"And what?" Grace said.

"They seem to be holding weapons," Watson replied.

Grace was sure Tom was just scared and that he wouldn't hurt anyone – he was just trying to protect himself from being taken away from his home.

"Then I'll have to go to the tower and speak to him," Grace said. "Watson, call Mum again and tell her to come to Eely Isle. Tell her about my plan."

Grace climbed up the outer section of the castle with her grappling hook and rope, making it onto the roof.

The tower was visible and Grace could see the robot puffins around the edge, holding what looked to be poles and spanners.

She'd faced all sorts as a warden so far, and it almost made her laugh to think she'd have to get past some small puffins.

Securing her rope, Grace climbed down the other side of the roof, crossed the courtyard, then took the path to the tower. She ran into the entrance and hurried up the spiral staircase inside until she could see the orange glow of dusk above.

But as she reached the opening to the rooftop, a puffin robot was waiting. It lunged at Grace with a spanner and she ducked just in time. It missed her head by a centimetre. "Hey!" she cried.

Then another puffin was by her feet, pulling at her ankles. Grace lost her footing and nearly fell back down the stairs, but she managed to grab the bannister and kick the bird away. "Tom, please. I just want to talk!" she called up.

Using all her energy, Grace darted past the puffin waving the spanner, thrust it aside and stepped onto the roof. At least twenty puffins were lined up before her. She could just see Tom behind them, grasping a control panel.

There was a click and all the puffins moved in formation. They were in an attacking position.

"Don't go any further," Tom called.

"Tom, this is silly!" Grace said. "Listen—"

Then the eyes of the puffins in the front row turned red. They stepped towards her and began performing leg sweeps, jabs and chops. It was such a strange sight that Grace was stunned for a moment and it took her a second to start fighting back.

One puffin had already chopped her knee and she fell forwards. She managed to grab the nearest puffin and pull its legs from beneath it. Then several puffins jumped on her back, pinning her down. "Hey! Get off!" Grace yelled.

"What in all of Moreland is going on?"

Grace turned her head to see her mum at the top of the staircase with Bren not far behind.

The puffins started attacking Mum and Bren too. Grace managed to pull the three puffins from her back and roll away, but only as another one jumped on her chest. It tried to hit her with a spanner and she moved her head so it just caught her ear.

Watson dived from above and chopped the back of the puffin's legs with his wing, sending

it flying off Grace's chest. Mum was battling six puffins and Bren was swarmed by another five when Grace saw her chance. She took a leap over the heads of three puffins between her and Tom, grabbed the controls off him and ripped out the power pack.

In an instant, the puffins all froze mid-action.

Grace blew a strand of her long brown hair from her face. "I'm not sure all this was needed," she said, rubbing her ear where the spanner had hit.

A tear trickled down Tom's cheek.

Grace sat beside him and pulled out her bag of jelly babies. "They're a bit squashed," she said, "but they'll still taste the same. Now, please let me tell you about my plan without setting a puffin army on me, because I think you might like it."

12

Family

Mum and Bren joined Grace, sitting down next to Tom on the roof. Grace explained her idea about letting Tom join them at Griffin House.

Mum looked at Grace and thought for a moment. "But the rule about keeping wardens in the family has been in place since—" Mum began.

"Great Grandma Griffin made the rule, I know," Grace said. "But are we really breaking the rule? Isn't family what we decide it to be? Tom had a family here in the orphanage. Amy

Eely was just like a mother to him before she died. Couldn't Tom become part of our family?"

Tom looked at Grace and blinked, his mouth wide open as if he couldn't believe what he was hearing. Another tear trickled down his cheek. Watson put a wing out to pass Tom a tissue.

"It's a good idea, Grace," Mum said. "You may be the youngest in the family, but you talk a lot of sense." She looked at Tom. "Would you like to visit Griffin House and see what you think? Grace is right. It's time to open up and extend the family."

Tom's eyes sparkled eagerly. The beginning of a smile was on his lips. "Really?" he said.

Ann Griffin nodded. "Really. But there's training involved, Tom. Would you be up for that?"

"Absolutely!" said Tom. "I'm a fast learner, but ..." He looked thoughtful and worried for a moment. "I'd miss Eely Isle."

Grace thought about how attached Tom was to the island and how he had many happy memories here. What if they made the portal on Eely Isle stronger and linked it to the map? Then they could pop back to the island any time and he wouldn't miss it. "Mum, what if Tom could come back to Eely Isle whenever he wanted?"

Ann paused, then smiled, realising what Grace meant. "I can take a look at your portal, Tom, and steady it with our teleport technology," she said. "Of course, we'll need to ensure that the portal technology is protected and used for good, not theft." She winked.

"And maybe we can help restore Eely Castle!" said Grace. In the short time she'd been on Eely Isle, she'd grown rather fond of it. She loved Copperport, but the island was a nice change from the hustle and bustle of the city.

"Thank you," Tom said, smiling. "I'd love to come and look at Griffin House."

Many months later, back in the map room of Griffin House, Grace pinned a warden badge onto Tom's uniform pocket. "There! How does it feel to be a fully trained warden?"

"It feels amazing!" Tom replied.

A new gate had been added to the Griffin map in the far northwest corner of Moreland, the location of Eely Isle. Grace activated the gate, took Tom's hand and in a flash of blue they both teleported. The castle was slowly being rebuilt to its former self and looked magnificent in the morning sun. Grace unwrapped the parcel she was carrying, revealing a bronze plate that read:

EELY CASTLE
SECOND HOME OF THE GRIFFIN WARDENS

"There," Grace said, hanging it by the door.

"Being a warden is great," said Tom. "But ..."

"But what?" said Grace, surprised. What could possibly be better than zooming between portals solving problems?

"But finding family is better," Tom finished.

Grace smiled. Then her pocket vibrated and she took out her flashing digi-com. It was Bren. "There's an emergency in Jackville," he said. "Something about the walking street lamps going crazy and taking over the town. Mum says it's all hands on deck."

"Tell her we're on our way," said Grace, then she turned to Tom. "Ready for your first proper mission?"

Tom nodded, his cheeks glowing and his blue eyes burning bright.

"Let's hope the street lamps haven't joined up with the robot puffins," Grace said, winking. She took the re-compass in one hand and Tom's hand in the other, and they spiralled away, teleporting in a flash of bright blue light.

In their NEXT adventure,
Grace and Tom
work TOGETHER to SOLVE

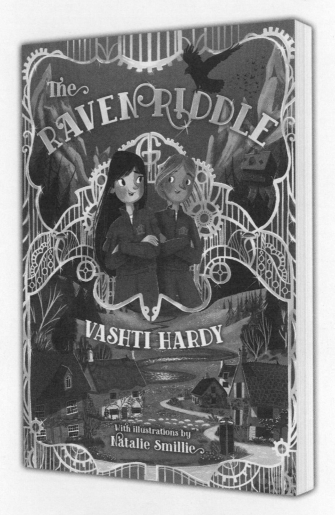

COMING SOON!